Fairy Unicorns

Wind Charm

Zanna Davidson

Illustrated by Nuno Alexandre Vieira

Meet the Unicorns

Zoe

Astra

Sorrel

Unicorn King

Tio

Orion

Lily

Shadow

Contents

Chapter One

Zoe waited until the clock struck midnight.
Then she crept out of her bedroom and tiptoed
down the stairs, her heart beating fast with
excitement. Feeling her way in the darkness,
she lifted the latch on the back door and
slipped out into the garden. The only sound
came from an owl, hooting in one of the far-off
fields. Zoe smiled. The silence and the stillness

had a kind of magic
to it. She loved staying
at her Great-Aunt May's
house – it was a place
full of wonderful
adventures…

As Zoe made
her way down
the garden,
she could see
the oak tree,
silhouetted
against the night
sky. With only the moonlight to guide her,
she picked her way towards it, and then,
when she stood beneath its arching branches,
she pulled a tiny silver bag from her pocket.

Zoe opened the bag as delicately as she could, and took out a pinch of sparkling, golden dust. She paused for a moment. Would the magic still work? Her fingers fizzing with excitement, she sprinkled the dust over herself as she chanted the words of a spell:

Let me pass into the magic tree,
Where *fairy unicorns fly* wild and *free.*
Show me the trail of sparkling light,
To Unicorn Island, shining bright.

All at once, Zoe felt a tingling feeling and she began to shrink, down, down, down, until she was fairy-sized. And there, between the roots of the oak tree, was a lighted tunnel, glimmering in the darkness.

"Oh!" she cried. "The magic still works. It's really happening!" She was on her way to Unicorn Island, a world full of Fairy Unicorns.

Zoe set off down the tunnel at a run, following the trail of light. The sandy floor of the oak tree felt warm beneath her bare feet. Then, with a gasp of wonder, she spotted the silvery branches of Unicorn Island, just visible at the end of the tunnel. "I'm coming! I'm coming!" she called, and with a final burst of speed, she came out of the tunnel and into the magical world.

She looked around in wonder. Unicorn Island was just as beautiful as she'd remembered. The silver bark of the trees glittered in the sunlight, their rainbow leaves a burst of colour against the clear blue sky. A moment later, a beautiful unicorn with a pearly horn came galloping out of the trees towards her. The unicorn's delicate wings fluttered gracefully in the breeze and her coat shone with silvery stars.

"Astra!" cried Zoe, flinging her arms around the unicorn's neck.

"You've come back," said Astra, her voice breathless with excitement. "I hoped you'd be here in time."

"In time for what?" asked Zoe.

In reply, Astra pushed her nose into a little

bag around her neck and pulled out a scroll,
tied with a velvet ribbon.

"Look at this," she said proudly.

Zoe unfurled the note and read:

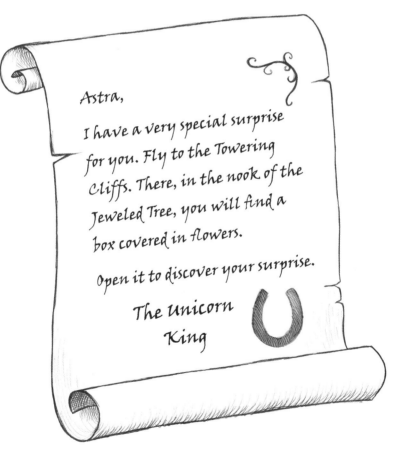

Astra,

I have a very special surprise
for you. Fly to the Towering
Cliffs. There, in the nook of the
Jeweled Tree, you will find a
box covered in flowers.

Open it to discover your surprise.

The Unicorn
King

"A messenger bird brought it to me this morning," Astra went on. "Isn't it exciting! It's like a treasure hunt."

"Wow!" said Zoe. "This must be your reward for your bravery against Shadow."

"Well, it should be for you too then," said Astra, smiling shyly at her. "We couldn't have defeated him without you."

Zoe was silent for a moment as she thought about the dangers they'd faced against Shadow, an evil pony from an island across the sea.

"But let's not think about Shadow today," said Astra, as if reading Zoe's mind. "There's too much to look forward to. Will you come with me to the Towering Cliffs?"

"Of course I will," said Zoe, slipping the scroll into her pocket, and untying the bag from Astra's neck.

"Thank you," said Astra. "I was going to show you the Island of Flowers. It's a beautiful place out in the Western Sea. No one lives there, but it's tended by the Flower Unicorns. Its soil is so fertile they grow the most amazing flowers there, and then use the leaves and petals in their spells. But I'll take you there afterwards. This is too exciting to wait."

Astra bent her legs and Zoe swung herself onto the unicorn's back.

"Where are the Towering Cliffs?" Zoe asked. "I've never heard of them before."

"They're not far from the Unicorn King's Castle," Astra replied. "It shouldn't take us long to get there. Let's hurry," she added with a grin, "and collect our surprise."

Chapter Two

Zoe and Astra cantered through the Silvery Glade, Astra's hoofs pounding over the soft ground.

"Shouldn't we tell your mother where we're going?" asked Zoe.

"She's not here," Astra replied. "She's at the Unicorn King's Castle with the other Guardians. They've been called together for an important meeting."

Zoe nodded in understanding. Astra's mother, Sorrel, was Guardian of the Trees. Along with the other Guardians, it was her job to help the King protect Unicorn Island.

"Besides," Astra went on, "I told her I was taking you to the Island of Flowers and we can go there after we've found the surprise. Now," she added, as they came out of the glade, "are you ready to fly?"

"I'm ready," said Zoe, though she felt a tingle of nerves rush through her. She loved soaring on Astra's back and seeing Unicorn Island from the air, but there was always that moment, as she looked down and saw the ground rushing away from her, when she couldn't help feeling a little afraid. "I just hope I remember how to do it," she added.

"You're a natural," said Astra, with a smile. "There's nothing to worry about. Now, hold tight!"

The next moment Astra began beating her wings, swishing them through the air in graceful arcs so that they rose into the sky.

"Oh!" gasped Zoe, as the grass disappeared from beneath her feet. She clung to Astra, pressing her cheek against her soft white coat.

"Are you okay?" asked Astra.

"Yes!" said Zoe. "It's just that it always takes my breath away."

But then she stretched out her arms, loving the way the warm breeze swept over her bare skin and ruffled her hair.

"Nothing is quite as magical as flying!"

Below her, Unicorn Island unfolded in all its beauty. The lush green valley came into view, with the sparkling Moon River winding across the valley floor.

"What about your magic, Astra?" Zoe asked tentatively. "Has it come back?"

When Zoe had first met Astra, she'd been the only unicorn on the island unable to do magic and Zoe knew how much it bothered her. But on her last visit, Astra had cast a powerful spell of her own for the very first time.

"No," said Astra, sadly. "I've tried but the magic just won't work again. I've been learning spells though," she added. "And maybe…now that you're here, it'll come back." She gave Zoe a small smile.

They sped across the island, following the azure path of Moon River. "Look!" Astra said at last. "We're nearly at the Towering Cliffs!"

Zoe looked up and saw the cliff face ahead of them. It was marble-white, gleaming in the sunshine. On outstretched wings, Astra rose up and over the clifftop and landed gracefully on the mossy ground at its peak. Zoe slid from her back and gasped.

"Wow!" she said. "You can see all over Unicorn Island from here."

For a moment Zoe gazed at the island, which sparkled like a jewel in the sun. Not far below them, she could see the Unicorn King's Castle, nestled majestically in the cliff face.

"Now we just need to find the Jeweled Tree," she said. She looked behind her at the line of trees, all foaming with beautiful blossoms. "How do we know which one it is?"

Beside her, Astra laughed. "Try again," she said. "Look closely."

Zoe scanned the trees once more, and gasped. There, in the middle, was a tree cut from clear crystal. It was a sight to behold. The sunlight glanced off it, creating dancing rainbows on the mossy ground. Instead of blossoms, its branches dripped with jewels – sapphires, emeralds and rubies. And halfway up its trunk was a little nook, in which Zoe could just make out a box, covered in flowers.

"What a strange tree," said Zoe. There was something eerie about its glittering stillness.

"I know," said Astra. "It was created by an old Guardian of the Spells, as proof of the power of his magic."

They walked towards its trunk, and Zoe reached up for the box. Just as the note had said, it was adorned in beautiful flowers – lilies, forget-me-nots and sweet peas – cascading from its lid like a flowery waterfall.

"Oh," said Zoe. "It's so pretty. I hardly want to pick it up in case I crush the flowers."

"Don't worry," said Astra, as Zoe took it from the nook and laid it on the ground. "You won't harm the flowers. It's sure to be enchanted. Oh! Isn't this a lovely surprise? I've never seen anything so pretty. You open it, Zoe. I'm so excited to find out what's inside."

"Thank you," said Zoe. She bent down, feeling anticipation rising within her.

"It is strange, though," Astra said with a frown. "There's something about this box. I feel like I know it somehow."

"Well, here goes," said Zoe. "We'll soon find out what it is." She reached for the clasp excitedly, but her heart began to pound, and her fingers shook as she began lifting the lid...

"Stop!" Astra cried suddenly. "Close the lid! I know what this is..."

But it was too late. The lid was opening, as if pushed by some invisible force. Try as she might, there was nothing Zoe could do to close it now. There was a rushing and roaring and a fierce wind burst out of the box. It spilled out in all directions and Zoe and Astra could only look on in horror as it raced across the island, tearing down everything in its path.

"What is it?" cried Zoe, battling to make her voice heard. "What have I done?"

"It's the Box of Winds," gasped Astra. "I remember it now – from the spell books! We've opened the Box of Winds, which unleashes a terrible storm. We have to stop it…or it's going to destroy the island!"

Chapter Three

Zoe and Astra watched in horror as the storm raged around them, worsening with every second. The winds were so strong now, Zoe could hardly stand. "I don't understand how this happened," she cried. "Do you think the King sent you the wrong box?"

"He couldn't have," Astra shouted back. "He wouldn't make a mistake like that.

I don't understand it either."

"We have to find shelter," gasped Zoe, "before this gets any worse." She picked up the empty box, though she couldn't see how they were going to get the winds back inside.

"We're not far from the Unicorn King's Castle," cried Astra. "Let's aim for that! Then we can tell him what's happened and get help."

Zoe looked down at the castle, just visible now in the swirling, dirt-filled air. "How will we get there?" she asked. "Is there a path?"

Astra shook her head. "We'll have to fly to reach it," she said, fighting to be heard against the wind. "There's no other way."

Zoe climbed back on to Astra, the Box of Winds tucked under one arm. With the other, she held Astra's neck tightly as the unicorn leaped into the air. Immediately, the wind caught them and they rocketed into the sky.

Zoe kept her body pressed flat against the warmth of Astra's back. It was all Astra could do to steer, as the wind tried its hardest to buffet them this way and that.

"I think landing is going to be tricky," cried Astra, as they neared the Unicorn King's Castle. "I'm going to aim for that ledge at the bottom, by the steps…"

Astra stretched out her wings to try to break their speed. For a terrifying moment, Zoe thought they were going to be dashed against the jagged rocks, but then they came spinning around to land, with a bump, beneath the castle steps.

"Whew," said Zoe, pushing her hair out of her eyes. "That was…adventurous."

"I know," said Astra, with a wobbly laugh. "Really scary! I just hope the Unicorn King knows how to stop this storm."

"Of course he will," said Zoe.

They raced up the steps to a pair of gleaming gates. Zoe pulled the bell rope hard, and inside they could just make out the sound of chiming bells over the roaring wind.

After what
seemed like an age,
the gates opened and a
small unicorn peered out. He
looked about the same age as
Astra, with a star in the middle
of his forehead, a scruffy mane
that stuck up in all directions and
an anxious, timid expression.

"Greetings!" he said. "And welcome to the Unicorn King's Castle. I am Tio, apprentice to Medwen, the new Guardian of the Spells. How may I help you?"

"Can you let us in?" said Astra. "I don't know if you've noticed, but there's a storm out here and it's getting worse by the moment."

Without waiting for an answer, Zoe and Astra rushed past him into the castle.

"At last," said Zoe, as Tio closed the gates. "We're out of the storm!"

Zoe put down the Box of Winds and gazed around the Unicorn King's Castle. Inside, the sound of the wind was muffled and the whole

castle seemed strangely silent after the noise
outside.

"Where is everyone?" asked Astra. "Where
are all the Castle Unicorns?"

"They're trying to stop the wind from
getting in," said Tio. "They're putting up the
shutters and battening down the roof."

Even as he spoke, two unicorns rushed past
him, with barely a glance in their direction.

"To the garden!" one cried. "We must
protect our herbs."

And with a clattering of hoofs they were
gone again, a distant castle door banging
shut behind them.

"Everyone's very busy," said Tio
importantly. "And I have to say," he added a
little huffily, "it's very unusual for a unicorn

and a human to rush in like this. May I
ask who you are?"

"I'm sorry," said Astra. "This is my friend
Zoe and I'm Astra, Sorrel's daughter. It's very
important that we see the King. Can
you take us to him?"

"Astra and Zoe?"
Tio repeated, his expression more
anxious than ever. "Oh no. I'm afraid you

can't see the King. You see, he's gone looking for you."

"I don't understand," said Zoe. "What do you mean?"

"Let me see," said Tio. "Not long ago… well maybe it was only ten minutes ago… No, I think it was more than that…"

He stopped, as if trying to work it out precisely. "Yes, let's say, fifteen minutes ago – I was just finishing my lunch. It was a very good lunch, actually—"

"Please, Tio," interrupted Astra. "Could you try telling us a little more quickly?"

For a moment, Tio looked offended and Zoe was worried he wasn't going to tell them anything. "Very well," he said at last. "I will keep it brief. As I was saying, not long ago, a message came from Shadow. He said he'd captured Astra and was holding her hostage. Sorrel said you'd gone to the Island of Flowers, beyond our shores. She went immediately to rescue you, and the King and the other Guardians went to help her. Only here you are…"

"Oh no!" groaned Astra. "This is worse than I thought." She turned to Tio, fear in her eyes. "This is Shadow's doing. You see, we've opened the Box of Winds."

"The Box of Winds?" Tio repeated. "This storm is from the Box of Winds?"

Astra nodded dumbly.

"B-but do you know what that is?" Tio stuttered. "It contains the most powerful and malevolent winds on the island. Their only aim is to destroy and it takes incredibly difficult magic to stop them. Why would you open it?"

"Because we were tricked," said Astra crossly. "I had a note from the Unicorn King, telling me to open it. Only I don't think it was from the King at all."

"Hang on," said Zoe. "I've still got it." She reached into her pocket and unrolled the parchment.

Together, they looked at the note and Zoe noticed that the shimmer of the King's hoof print had begun to fade.

"Oh yes," said Tio. "That's a forgery! The King's hoof print never fades."

"I had no idea," said Astra. "A bird brought it to me and…"

"Of course – Shadow would have sent any message by bird, as he's banished from the island," Tio pointed out. "It's a very clever

trick, but I'm surprised you didn't realize."

"Well it's obvious now, isn't it," snapped Astra.

Zoe could see the tension mounting between Astra and Tio and was about to step in and say something, when a fresh whooshing noise came from outside. It sounded as if the wind was hurtling around the castle, desperately trying to find a way in. They all rushed over to the window.

"The storm's getting worse," said Zoe. "If

we don't do something to stop the winds soon, they'll destroy everything on the island."

"This must be Shadow's plan," gasped Astra. "If the island is ruined, then the King will have failed in his role to protect it…and Shadow will be free to take over."

"Yes," said Tio, nodding. "That's Unicorn Law: any King who fails to protect the island must give up his crown."

"But the King and the Guardians will soon realize we're not on the Island of Flowers," Zoe pointed out. "Then they'll come back and stop the storm."

"It takes a long time to get to the Island of Flowers," said Astra. "It's some way from our shores. I don't think we can wait for them."

"Oh!" cried Zoe. "This is all my fault for

opening the box. I'm so sorry. I'll do anything to make this right."

"It's not your fault," said Astra gently. "We were both tricked by Shadow. But you're right – now we have to find a way to stop the winds before it's too late for the island, and the King!"

Chapter Four

Astra, Zoe and Tio stood together in tense silence. All around them, the sound of the wind seemed to grow stronger, as if at any moment it might rip off the castle roof and dash it against the rocks below.

"What about the other unicorns?" asked Zoe. "We could gather them together to help."

But Astra shook her head. "The unicorns

here help look after the castle – they wouldn't
have the magic to stop a storm like this. And
no one on the island will be leaving their
homes – not with such a strong wind."

Zoe could see that Astra's eyes were welling
with tears. "If only I could do magic," the
little unicorn whispered beneath her breath.

In desperation, Zoe turned to Tio. "Didn't
you say you were apprentice to the new
Guardian of the Spells?" she asked. "Do you
know a way to stop the storm?"

But Tio only looked at her doubtfully. "It
would take a very complicated spell to stop
this storm," he said.

"But you have spell books here," insisted
Astra. "Can't we look in them?"

"Well, no, not really," said Tio. "Only the

Guardian of the Spells and the Unicorn King are allowed in the Spell Room. And I'm only supposed to go in with one of them."

"This is an emergency!" said Zoe. "If we don't stop the wind, the island will be destroyed. Please, Tio, let us use the Spell Room."

"But I never break the rules," said Tio, as if he were speaking to himself. "Oh dear, maybe just this once... Come on," he sighed. He began trotting off down one of the corridors, beckoning them to follow.

It seemed to Zoe as if he led them down a
maze of corridors. She had had no idea the
castle was so huge. It was as if they were going
right back into the heart of the rock face. But
at last they came to an arched doorway,
sealed shut with a thick wooden door that was
covered in brass studs. Zoe noticed there was
no handle on the door, no keyhole.

Tio glanced around at them. "Step back a moment, please," he said. "This spell is secret."

Then he began muttering words beneath his breath until, with a loud creak, the door swung open. All three of them stepped inside.

The room was lined from floor to ceiling with books. The only other object was a table, inlaid with a map of Unicorn Island.

The feeling of magic crackled in the air.

"Okay," said Zoe, taking a deep breath. "Let's get to work right away. Where should we look?"

Even as she spoke she heard a howling sound, as if the wind was hurrying down the corridors. The heavy door began banging open and shut behind them, and Astra quickly ran to close it.

"Tio, tell us, where should we look?" said Zoe urgently.

"Let me think a moment," said Tio.

Astra and Zoe waited in agonized silence while Tio perused the shelves. "Yes," he said at last. "The middle three shelves on the left. Those are the spell books for wind and weather. If there's a spell to stop this storm, it'll be there."

They set to work at once, taking down book after book from the shelves, frantically flipping through the pages for a spell to calm the winds. Zoe tried to ignore the cold breeze that snaked its way under the door and swirled around her feet, and the echo of doors banging in distant parts of the castle. She scanned the pages as fast as she could, but there were so many books to get through.

Zoe was just starting to panic when she heard a cry from Astra. "I think I've got it!" she said. "Here! Come and look at this!"

They gathered around a huge spell book, its pages yellowed with age. At the top of the page Zoe read *The Box of Winds* and just beneath it there was a drawing of the box they had found, covered in flowers.

"Yes!" Zoe cried. "It's just the same."

She read the words of the spell. "That sounds simple enough," she said. "What happens now? Do we just go outside and say it?"

Tio shook his head. "It says we need the box, or we'll never get the winds to return. Do you still have it?"

Zoe looked around, confused for a moment. "Oh!" she said. "I left it just inside the gates, when we first arrived at the castle."

"We need more than the Box of Winds," said Astra, reading on. "Listen to this: *The spell will capture the winds and draw them back into the box, but first the winds must be made to listen, and they won't listen to words alone. They need music."*

"What kind of music?" asked Zoe.

"I remember now!" said Tio. "The Flower Unicorns control the breezes. That's why the box is covered with flowers: it's a symbol that the winds are in their control. And the Flower Unicorns make the most magical music on the island. We must go to them and ask for help."

"Great," said Astra. "We've got a plan."

But Tio had suddenly turned very pale. "Oh crumbs," he said, gulping. "That means going out into the storm – all the way to the Flower Meadows."

"But will the Flower Unicorns be there?" asked Zoe.

"There are caves at the edges of the meadows," Astra replied. "The Flower Unicorns have probably taken shelter there."

"Then what are we waiting for?" said Zoe. "Let's go!"

They turned to leave, but Tio hung back.

"Come on, Tio," said Zoe, seeing him hesitate.

"Ah," said Tio, "well, you see, I should really stay here, and, um, guard the Spell Room. Or practice my spells. Yes, I should definitely practice my spells."

"It's okay to be scared, Tio," said Astra.

Tio refused to meet her eyes. "Here's the spell to capture the winds," he said, hurriedly copying it out. "Well then, good luck!" he added. "I'll be here when you get back…"

"So you're really staying here?" said Astra, her gentle voice sounding sterner than Zoe had ever heard it.

Tio nodded. Zoe swung herself on to Astra's back, but, suddenly, she couldn't help herself. "Tio," she said. "You must come. I can't even do magic and I'm going, and Astra's magic doesn't always work. We need your help. Think of the island!"

Zoe waited tensely, wondering if she'd gone too far. A range of expressions flitted across Tio's face, as if he was struggling to decide what to do. But then, at last, he nodded. "Fine," he said. "I'll come with you to find the Flower Unicorns. But that's as far as I go."

As he spoke, he began putting on two large saddlebags, each full to the brim with books.

The bags looked so heavy, Zoe was surprised he didn't topple over.

"What are those for?" she asked.

"They're my spell books. I never fly anywhere without them."

Zoe and Astra looked at each other for a brief moment, then grinned.

"Ready?" asked Astra.

"Ready," said Tio and Zoe in unison.

They galloped back through the castle, and as they reached the gates, Zoe bent down and snatched up the Box of Winds.

Then they charged out through the gates into the storm once more.

"Here goes," said Astra, as the wind whipped through her mane, and she launched herself into the air, with Zoe astride her back. With a gasp, Tio followed close behind them.

But this time, the storm was too strong for them. No sooner had Astra left the stone steps than she was driven back, as if the wind was refusing to let her leave. Zoe could just make out Tio ahead of them, battling through the storm clouds, clearly unaware he'd left them behind.

"I can't do it," said Astra, tears of frustration in her eyes. "I need to be able to do magic. Only a spell will see us through this storm. We'll just have to wait for Tio to come back for us."

"You *can* do magic," said Zoe. "It's happened before; it will happen again. Stay calm. Think of a spell. We can do this together."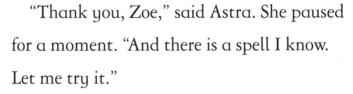

"Thank you, Zoe," said Astra. She paused for a moment. "And there is a spell I know. Let me try it."

She collected herself then began to chant:

Through the gusts and through the gale,
Guard my flight, so I won't fail.
Lead me to the place I seek,
Make me strong where I was weak.

"Astra!" Zoe cried. "I think the magic is working. The stars on your coat are glowing. Can you feel it?"

"Yes, I can!" Astra shouted back. "I really can. I've got that same fizzing in my hoofs and in my wings. Let me try again. Hold tight."

This time, when Astra launched herself into the air, they raced through the wind, cutting through the storm like a scythe.

"You did it, Astra!" cried Zoe. "We're going to make it to the Flower Unicorns. Your magic has come back!"

Astra smiled. "Now, we must find the Flower Meadows. It's grown so dark I can hardly see where I'm going. Where's Tio?"

"Down there!" cried Zoe, suddenly. "To your left. He's waiting for us near the bank of the river. Oh!" she added. "I've never seen Moon River like that before."

The water was mesmerizing to watch – usually so calm and placid, it was frothing and heaving in the wind.

Astra swept down until they were resting on the bank next to Tio, standing a little way back from the churning waves.

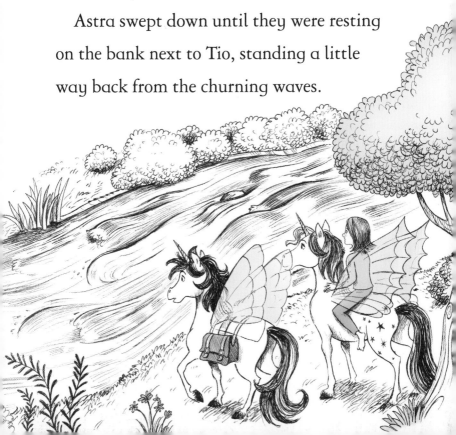

"I thought I'd lost you," Tio shouted over the storm. "Let's get to the caves."

They began galloping across the meadows in the direction of the hills. The valley floor, usually carpeted in flowers, was now empty and bare. Instead the air was thick with torn petals, rushing this way and that on the vicious gusts.

"Almost there," said Astra, as the caves came into view.

"We're going to make it," Zoe whispered to herself. "We might just be able to save the island…"

Chapter Five

Astra galloped the last stretch at full pelt, passing Tio as they neared the entrance to the caves.

"Come on, Tio," called Zoe.

Then she saw that Tio was standing still, with his eyes shut, as if suddenly overcome with fear. "Tio," she said urgently. "We'll be safe in the cave."

At the word "safe," Tio's eyes sprang open and, without a word, he followed them until they were inside the dark mouth of the cave.

Outside, the wind was still rushing and roaring, but it whooshed past the cave entrance. "Oh!" said Zoe. "It's so quiet in here. I can hear myself think again."

She slid from Astra's back, and as
her eyes adjusted to the dim light,
she saw a group of Flower Unicorns
approaching them. One wore a beautiful
circlet of delicate flowers, and Zoe
recognized her as Lily, Guardian of
the Flowers.

Her expression was one of concern and surprise. "Thank goodness you're safe," she said. "We thought you were being held captive on the Island of Flowers?"

At this Astra shook her head, and Lily went on, "Do you know what's happening? We've been trying, and failing, to control the winds. We fear this is Shadow's work."

"It is," said Zoe. "He fooled us…into opening the Box of Winds."

"No!" cried Lily. "It can't be."

In answer, Zoe held out the box, her hands still trembling slightly with fright. "I'm afraid it is," she said.

"After it happened, we went to find the Unicorn King," added Astra. "But Shadow tricked him into going to the Island of Flowers.

My mother's there too, along with some of the other Guardians."

"I know. I was there – at the castle," said Lily. "The Guardians of the Clouds, Snow, Forest and Spells all went with him to find you. I came back here. The King wanted one of us to stay behind, to look after the island. But I never imagined this would happen…"

"We've found the spell to call back the winds," said Zoe. "But the winds won't listen to words alone – we need your music. Will you help?"

"Of course," said Lily. "It all makes sense now why our wind spells weren't working."

She stared out into the storm again. "If only we had time, we could go to the Island of Flowers and call back the King and the

Guardians. We may not be able to defeat the storm without their help."

"But we have to try or Shadow will take over the island," said Astra.

"We will use our music to help," said Lily. "I'll call together the rest of my unicorns. Many of them are sheltering at the back of the cave. Wait here, while we gather our instruments."

Without another word, she turned, and disappeared into the shadows.

"I hope this works," said Zoe.

"Me too," Astra replied. "This is our only hope to stop the storm."

They looked over at Tio, who had stayed silent ever since they had reached the cave. He was still quivering in shock.

"Are you okay, Tio?" Zoe asked gently.

"Don't like adventures," mumbled Tio. "Next time you two come knocking at the castle door, I'm going to keep the gates firmly shut."

Zoe and Astra exchanged smiles. Then from deep inside the cave behind them came unicorn after unicorn, each carrying an instrument. There were harps made from willow, wooden flutes and harmonicas, seashell horns and reed pipes. The unicorns gathered by the entrance to the cave, their beautiful butterfly wings fluttering in the wind.

"Oh!" said Zoe, turning anxiously to Astra. "This is it, isn't it – our only chance?"

Astra nodded. "If this doesn't calm the winds, nothing will."

Zoe crossed her fingers. She couldn't bear to think what would happen if the spell and the music failed to work.

Then, at a nod from Lily, the Flower Unicorns took up their instruments and began to play.

At first, the music was only a faint sound against the roar of the wind, but it was still more beautiful than anything Zoe had heard before. It sounded like the song of the wind itself.

"It's time to chant the spell," said Lily. "The storm is growing stronger all the time,

and we must say it soon, or we'll never be able to call back the winds. It's an ancient spell, but it is complicated and requires powerful magic. I will need your help. Zoe, have you got the Box of Winds?"

Zoe held out the box to her.

"Hold it open," said Lily. "If the spell works, the winds should come rushing in. And whatever you do, don't let go. If we lose the box, we've lost all hope of capturing the storm."

"Now, Astra and Tio," Lily went on, "are you ready to say the spell with me?"

"My…my magic doesn't always work," Astra replied, her voice wavering.

"But last time it worked with me by your side," Zoe whispered to her. "I'll say the words with you."

"Thank you," Astra whispered back. Then she turned to Lily and took a deep breath. "I'm ready," she said.

Zoe passed them the words of the spell, and they all began to chant it together, over and over, their voices rising and twining with the sound of the music:

North, south, east and west,
Winds turned wild, come to rest.
Listen to our soothing song,
Come back home, where you belong.

At first, nothing seemed to be happening and Zoe was worried their voices would never be heard over the roar of the storm. "Louder," cried Lily. "We need to say it louder."

They chanted it again and again, their
voices bellowing now, as if doing battle with
the wind. Lily's voice rang true and strong
and Zoe noticed Astra's voice swell with
strength. Glancing over, she saw the silver
stars on her coat were glowing more brightly
than they ever had before, and Zoe knew
Astra's magic was stirring again.

"Oh!" she cried out. "I think it's working."
It seemed to Zoe as if the winds were calming

and she held the box tight,

ready for them to return.

But to her dismay,

nothing seemed to be

happening. Looking

over, Zoe could see the

Flower Unicorns

playing harder than ever, their lilting music mingling with the wind, but their call wasn't tempting the racing winds back into the box.

"What's going on?" asked Zoe.

"Our magic isn't strong enough," said Astra, breathless from her chanting. "We need more help."

"We can do it!" said Lily. "We've calmed the winds. We can tempt them back. Keep chanting."

They sang out the words of the spell until their voices were hoarse, but Zoe could only watch in despair as she saw the winds sweep across the island, while the box lay empty in her hands.

"It really isn't working," she said, a sob rising in her throat.

"No," added Astra brokenly. "What do we do now?"

Lily hung her head. "Close the box, Zoe," she said, almost in a whisper, exhausted from the spell. "You're right. Without the King and the other Guardians, we don't have the power to return the winds to the box, only to still the storm a little."

Lily stopped speaking for a moment and sighed in defeat. "We're going to have to find

the King and the Guardians. We can't do this without their help. And we must hurry. We'll only be able to hold the winds at bay for so long. After that, they'll tear the island apart...until it's completely destroyed."

Zoe and Astra looked out anxiously across the island as Lily went on.

"I'll have to stay here with the Flower Unicorns. We must keep playing the music and chanting the spell so that we don't lose all control of the winds. It will take all our strength... I cannot spare anyone. And that leaves me with no choice... For the sake of the island, I must ask you three to go to the Island of Flowers to find the King."

Tio gulped. "All of us?" he said.

"All of you," said Lily. "There's safety in

numbers. I don't know what you'll find there…it seems very strange to me that the King hasn't yet returned. I wouldn't ask you to go, but we're desperate. The island is in grave danger. Do you know the way?"

"Yes," said Astra bravely. "We'll go immediately."

Zoe thought proudly how Astra hadn't hesitated, even for a moment.

"You can travel safely through this cave," Lily went on. "It reaches all the way back to the western edge of the island, where the cliffs meet the sea. Then you must fly west until you reach the Island of Flowers."

Chapter Six

Zoe climbed on to Astra's back and they began trotting through the cave. "Be safe!" called out the Flower Unicorns. "Good luck!" And then their chiming voices were drowned out as the cave filled with the sound of their music once more.

"How will we see where we're going?" asked Zoe.

The deeper they went into the cave, the darker it became.

In reply, Tio muttered a spell, and the next moment a shining trail of light began to spill across the cave floor, showing them the way.

"I'm really not happy about this," Tio muttered beneath his breath.

Zoe looked at him anxiously, half-fearing

that he would turn back. "What is it?" she asked. "What are you worried about?"

"I've been thinking," he said. "The Island of Flowers... It's just beyond the boundaries of Unicorn Island."

"What does that mean?" asked Zoe.

"The Unicorn King's banishment spell will still work there," replied Tio. "But Shadow and Orion might be able to use their magic. What if they've cast a spell on the Island of Flowers?"

"Oh no!" said Astra, and Zoe could tell she was thinking about her mother, while Tio looked longingly back the way they'd come.

"But we have to go," said Zoe. "If we don't, the storm will only wreak more damage."

"I know you're right," said Tio, reluctantly. Then, with a toss of his head, he broke into a gallop, clearly set on finishing this mission as fast as he could.

After that, they galloped side by side, until they reached the end of the tunnel, where it opened out onto the cliff face. Below them they could see the pounding waves of the Western Sea.

Tio looked straight ahead at the afternoon sun, and Zoe could feel the tension rising, as they all wondered

what they would find when they arrived at the Island of Flowers.

"Right," said Tio. "Time to fly." The unicorns spread their wings and took to the air, soaring over the churning waves. Zoe held tight to Astra as the wind whipped through her hair.

She scanned the horizon, while Tio and Astra beat their wings as fast as they could, speeding them over the sea.

They flew on and on, the sinking sun marking the time. Then, just as the afternoon light began to fade, Zoe saw a blaze of color in the water ahead of them.

"Oh!" she cried suddenly. "Is that it?"

"Yes, that's it," said Astra, her voice filled with relief. "Not long now. I hope my mother is safe, and the others."

As they drew nearer, the island became clearer. It was a perfect oval that seemed to float on the water. Its entire surface was thick with flowers and their sweet scent washed over the waves towards Zoe and her friends.

Soon, Tio and Astra began to swoop down, until they landed on the mossy banks at the very edge of the island.

Zoe gasped as she slid from Astra's back. She hadn't realized from the air how tall the flowers were – many were the size of trees. She gazed up at the huge, blooming petals looming overhead. It was like being in a jungle and, this close, the smell of the

flowers was almost overpowering.

"I was hoping we could fly over the island and spot the King and the Guardians from the air," said Astra. "But the flowers are too high and thick for that. We'd never be able to see them."

"Look!" Zoe cried suddenly. "What's this?"

She reached out her hand and plucked a wreath that was hanging from one of the stems. It was woven with ivy, bluebells and passion flowers.

"It's my mother's circlet!" said Astra, with a gasp. "They must have come this way. She never takes it off." She scanned the thick flowers. "Over there!" she cried. "I can see a path through the flowers. It looks like it's been freshly made."

They cantered over to the beginning of a narrow path between the stems.

"I'm sorry," said Tio behind them, his voice shaking slightly. "But I just can't do it... I can't go with you!"

Astra and Zoe turned. "It's all right, Tio," said Astra. "Thank you for coming this far."

"Will you wait for us here?" asked Zoe.

Tio nodded. "I won't leave without you. I promise. But..." he began, then gulped. "I'm just not brave enough to go any further."

Zoe smiled at him, and then, with her heart pounding in her chest, she began running down the path through the flowers, Astra galloping ahead.

The further they went, the thicker the air

became, as if it were drenched in the scent of the flowers. The path wound this way and that, and soon it was so narrow, they could only move slowly along it.

"I hope we find the King and the Guardians soon," said Astra. "I can't help feeling something must be very wrong if my mother has lost her circlet."

Zoe gazed at the sky, desperate for some sign of the other unicorns. Then she realized that Astra's pace was slowing. Finally the unicorn stopped dead on the path in front of her.

"Astra!" said Zoe. To her horror, she saw that Astra's eyes were beginning to close, her legs bending as she sank to the ground. "What are you doing? You look like you're about to fall asleep!"

"I'm just so tired," said Astra, with a yawn. She began rolling onto her side, her legs stretched out in front of her.

"You can't go to sleep! We haven't found the King yet. Or the Guardians," Zoe cried.

But Astra's eyes were closed. From her heavy breathing, it sounded as if she were sleeping.

Zoe began to shake her awake. "Please, Astra," she begged. "Please! Wake up!"

Astra's eyes flickered open. "Can't..." she said drowsily. "Must be a spell... Sleep...spell."

"But I don't feel tired," said Zoe.

"No," said Astra, closing her eyes again. "The spell wouldn't work on you...only on... unicorns..."

On those words, she closed her eyes, and didn't open them again. "Astra!" Zoe cried, but this time there was no answer. In a panic, Zoe stumbled on down the path. She had a horrible feeling she now had the answer as to why the Unicorn King hadn't returned. And she didn't have to go far before she was proved right. Ahead of her, in a little clearing

among the flowers, lay the Unicorn King
and the Guardians, all in a deep sleep, just
like Astra.

Zoe went to the King first, gently pulling
on his golden mane. "Please wake up!" she
cried. "We need you."

He didn't respond to her cries and she ran to each of the Guardians in turn, desperately trying to shake them awake, but the spell held all the unicorns in its thrall.

"Oh no," she cried aloud. "We'll never stop the storm now."

She sat down for a moment in despair, with her head in her hands. She felt powerless. She had no magic, no wings with which to fly for help. All she could do was sit here and wait for another unicorn to come, and all the while, Shadow would be ever closer to destroying the island.

But then a thought came to her – she wasn't alone. Tio was still at the edge of the island. There was a chance he hadn't been affected by the spell.

She ran back down the narrow path as fast as she could, pushing away the heavy flowers that blocked her way. To her relief, there was Tio, just where they'd left him, anxiously waiting on the mossy bank.

"It's a sleeping spell," said Zoe, in a breathless rush. "Shadow must have cast a sleep spell over the island. It's affected Astra and I found the King and the

Guardians, all asleep as well."

Tio began backing away. "Then there's nothing we can do," he said. "We'll have to go back and tell the others...gather everyone together... I can't go any further on to the island. I'd fall asleep too and then who would wake me?"

"No, Tio," said Zoe urgently. "We can't run away. Look in your saddlebags. You're loaded down with spell books. You must be able to work out a way to break the sleeping spell. If we leave now it could be too late – for everyone, and for Unicorn Island."

Tio paused for a moment, and Zoe had no idea what he was going to say. Then he took a deep breath. "Okay," he said at last. "I'll try."

In a flash, he rummaged in his saddlebags

and began flicking
through his spell
books as fast
as he could.
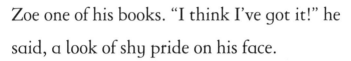
A moment
later he passed
Zoe one of his books. "I think I've got it!" he
said, a look of shy pride on his face.

"Will it work if you say it from here?"

"I don't know," said Tio, looking
despondent for a moment.

"If only Astra were awake," said Zoe. "She's
always brilliant at working things out."

At that, Tio puffed up once more. "Astra's
not the only clever unicorn on the island," he
said. "I'm sure this will work." And he began
to chant:

Wind so strong, wild and free,
Carry this spell on the breeze for me.
Wake the unicorns from their sleep,
Raise them from their slumbers deep.

Zoe was amazed to hear how Tio's voice changed as he chanted the spell. It sounded deeper, more serious. There was no anxiety on his face now, only a look of concentration as he said the words over and over.

Zoe watched in wonder as sparkling silver stars streamed out from Tio's horn. They were carried by the breeze down the tangled path and then disappeared among the flowers.

They both waited to see what would happen, their eyes fixed on the path ahead. "Please work, please work," whispered Zoe.

But there was no sound, and the path stayed just as it was, thick with flowers and with no sign of any unicorn.

"How long should the spell take to work?" asked Zoe.

"I don't know," said Tio, looking as worried as Zoe felt. "I've never said this spell before..."

"Wait!" cried Zoe, holding up her hand. "What's that?" Hearing a rustling among the leaves, she rushed forward, only to see a small bird flit between the flower stems.

"Oh!" she said, her voice flooding with disappointment as she turned to Tio. "I thought..."

But Tio lifted his head, his ears pricked. "Look up!" he cried.

The Unicorn King soared above the flowers

in a flash of golden light. Behind him came
the Guardians of the Snow, Clouds and Spells,
their translucent wings beating in time. And
last of all, with relief, Zoe saw Astra at her
mother's side. Sorrel, Guardian of the Forest,
was gazing across at her daughter as if she
never wanted to let her go.

They fluttered down to
land beside Zoe and Tio.

"It worked!"
cried Tio. "My
spell really
worked!"

The Unicorn
King reared up beside them, his golden horn
flashing in the fading light. He nodded at
them both. "Tio," he said, his voice solemn

and wise. "It was your spell then, that woke us from our deep sleep?"

Tio could only nod in reply.

"Thank you," said the King. "What has happened here today?"

"Shadow has struck again," began Zoe. She could see that Astra was still groggy with sleep, so she continued with the story. "He tricked us into opening the Box of Winds, and now a storm is raging across the island. The Flower Unicorns are trying to control it, but we need your help."

"I see," said the King. "That explains why Shadow sent us a message, pretending to have kidnapped you. He wanted us out of the way. Well, his plans have failed. We will return to Unicorn Island now and stop the storm. We

cannot wait a moment longer. Follow us as
fast as you can."

In a flash, the King and the other
Guardians were gone, the strength of
their magic driving them
like lightning across
the sky.

"Thank you,"
said Astra, smiling
at Tio. "You saved us. You had courage when
it counted."

But at her words, Tio's look of pride vanished and he hung his head.

"It wasn't me who saved you," he said. "Not really. I wanted to run away. It was Zoe who persuaded me to stay."

"But you didn't run," said Zoe, putting her arms around him. "Now let's go and see the King and the Guardians defeat Shadow's storm!"

Chapter Seven

Astra, Zoe and Tio soared over the sea, the
churning waters throwing up great gusts of
spray. Ahead of them, they could see
Unicorn Island still in the grip of the storm.
The trees on the clifftops were almost
snapping under the strength of the wind and
the air was thick with sticks and stones and
clods of earth.

"Maybe we should go back through the cave," suggested Zoe.

"Definitely," said Tio. "I don't think my nerves can take the wind any more."

They flew straight to the cave's entrance and galloped down its twisting pathway, their breathing heavy and tired now. At the other end they saw Lily and the Flower Unicorns, still playing their beautiful music. Beyond them, standing proud, were the King and the other Guardians, chanting the words of the spell.

"Oh!" cried Astra. "Look! They're taming the last of the winds."

Even as they watched, they sensed the winds grow quieter. First the stones, then the leaves and last of all the dust came to rest on

the ground and Lily closed the Box of Winds
with a snap.

"Oh! It's done," said Lily, her voice flooded
with relief.

"I'm so sorry we ever opened it," Zoe
blurted out.

The King looked over at them. "Shadow
tricked you," he said. "You mustn't feel
responsible. And without you, we never could
have captured the winds again." His gaze

took in all three of them. "Tio, Astra and Zoe," he said solemnly, "thank you, for everything you've done."

Zoe smiled up at the King, but as she looked beyond the cave at the valley, her feeling of relief vanished.

"But the island is ruined," she gasped. "So much has been destroyed." She felt tears well up in her eyes as she took in the scene.

Trees were strewn across the valley floor. She could see the unicorns' beautiful log cabins were missing roofs and doors, and the ground was covered in huge boulders that must have cascaded down from the mountain tops. The Flower Meadows were flooded and all around them torn petals lay forlornly on the ground.

"Don't worry," said the Unicorn King. "All this can be remedied with magic." As he spoke, he flew up into the air, his majestic wings glinting in the sunlight. "Come," he said to the Guardians. They all joined him in the sky and began to chant:

> Broken trees and windswept flowers,
> We give to you our healing powers.
> Ravaged earth and wind-torn skies,
> Restore yourselves and hear our cries:
> The storm is over, the danger passed,
> Unicorn Island has peace at last.

"Astra, Zoe," the King called down. "We need your help too."

Astra fluttered up into the sky, Zoe astride

her back. As they spoke the words of the spell, the silver stars on Astra's back began to glow brightly. Around them, the storm's destruction was slowly but surely being reversed. Fallen trees rose from the ground, while petals stirred on the magical breeze and took to the air in a rainbow wave before settling back upon the flowers. Grassy roofs lifted from the ground and floated back down to rest gently on the log cabins. Soon, Unicorn Island looked as beautiful as ever.

There was a moment of quiet, and then slowly, tentatively, the unicorns emerged from their hiding places. Some came out of their log cabin houses, others crept out of caves they had hidden in for safety, or from deep inside the woods.

They all gathered together in the Flower
Meadows and the Unicorn King addressed
them. "The storm is over," he declared.
"Shadow tricked us into unleashing the Box of
Winds and cast a sleep spell over myself and
the Guardians. But once again we have
defeated his evil plans!"

At this, a great cheer went up from the
unicorns, and then Lily, Guardian of the
Flowers, fluttered over until she was hovering
beside the King.

"And to celebrate the end of the storm, let
us all dance together in the Flower Meadows!"

At this, an even louder cheer went up.

Astra, Zoe and Tio looked at each other and grinned.

The Flower Unicorns took up their instruments once more and soon the valley was filled with the sound of their music and the sight of dancing unicorns.

Astra, Zoe and Tio hung back a moment just to watch, as the unicorns galloped and pranced in time to the music, weaving and circling, tossing their heads and swishing their tails. Then Astra smiled at her friends. "Let's dance!" she said.

"I'm not really a dancing unicorn," Tio began, but Zoe just laughed. "Just this once," she said, and soon they were dancing together in the warm evening air.

Zoe felt like she could stay forever, but as darkness gathered in the skies above them and the valley was lit by shining stars, Sorrel beckoned to her and Astra.

"Night is drawing in," she said, "and it is time for Zoe to return to her world. Astra, will you fly her to the entrance to the Great Oak?"

"Of course," said Astra, smiling.

"And, Zoe," Sorrel went on, "like the King, I want to thank you for everything you did today. Without you, I might not have Astra back at my side."

"But I didn't do anything…" protested Zoe.

"You have helped more than you know," Sorrel said softly.

Then Zoe slipped her arms around Astra's neck and waved goodbye to Sorrel. As they

leaped into the air, ready to take flight, they
saw that Tio had left the dance to join them.

"Thank you for making me say that spell,"
called Tio. "When you come back, will you
visit me at the castle?"

"Yes!" Zoe called back, grinning. "And then we can have more adventures together."

"I think tea and cake would be better," Tio replied.

Zoe laughed and gave a final wave, as Astra began beating her wings harder, powering them up, up into the sky. As they flew, the Flower Unicorns' beautiful music followed them on the warm evening breeze.

Zoe gazed down at Unicorn Island. The Moon River glittered beneath them, and the branches of the Silvery Glade waved them on.

All too soon, they reached the entrance to the Great Oak. Zoe slid from Astra's back and gave her one last hug.

"Promise you'll come again soon?" asked Astra.

"I promise," said Zoe. "Just try and keep me away!"

With one last wave, she began running back down the tunnel towards her own world. And even as she ran, Zoe was dreaming of her next magical adventures on Unicorn Island.

Edited by Becky Walker

Designed by Brenda Cole

Reading consultant: Alison Kelly

First published in 2017 by Usborne Publishing Ltd.,
Usborne House, 83-85 Saffron Hill, London EC1N 8RT, England.
www.usborne.com

This edition first published in America in 2018

Front cover and inside illustrations by Nuno Vieira Alexandre

The name Usborne and the devices ♛ 🎈 are Trade Marks of
Usborne Publishing Ltd.

This is a work of fiction. The characters, incidents, and dialogues are products of the author's
imagination and are not to be construed as real. Any resemblance to actual events or persons,
living or dead, is entirely coincidental.

A CIP catalogue record for this book is available from the British Library.